AWESOME ANIMALS IN THEIR HABITATS

PROTECTING RAIN FOREST ANIMALS

LAUREN KUKLA

Consulting Editor, Diane Craig, M.A./Reading Specialist

Sandcastle

An Imprint of Abdo Publishing
abdopublishing.com

abdopublishing.com

Published by Abdo Publishing, a division of ABDO, PO Box 398166, Minneapolis, Minnesota 55439. Copyright © 2017 by Abdo Consulting Group, Inc. International copyrights reserved in all countries. No part of this book may be reproduced in any form without written permission from the publisher. SandCastle™ is a trademark and logo of Abdo Publishing.

Printed in the United States of America, North Mankato, Minnesota

102016
012017

THIS BOOK CONTAINS RECYCLED MATERIALS

Editor: Rebecca Felix
Content Developer: Nancy Tuminelly
Cover and Interior Design and Production: Mighty Media, Inc.
Photo Credits: Ferenc Szelepcsenyi/Shutterstock Images, Shutterstock Images

Publisher's Cataloging-in-Publication Data

Names: Kukla, Lauren, author.
Title: Protecting rain forest animals / by Lauren Kukla.
Description: Minneapolis, MN : Abdo Publishing, 2017. | Series: Awesome animals in their habitats
Identifiers: LCCN 2016944678 | ISBN 9781680784299 (lib. bdg.) | ISBN 9781680797824 (ebook)
Subjects: LCSH: Animals--Habitations--Juvenile literature. | Habitat (Ecology)--Juvenile literature. | Wildlife conservation--Juvenile literature.
Classification: DDC 577--dc23
LC record available at http://lccn.loc.gov/2016944678

SandCastle™ Level: Transitional

SandCastle™ books are created by a team of professional educators, reading specialists, and content developers around five essential components—phonemic awareness, phonics, vocabulary, text comprehension, and fluency—to assist young readers as they develop reading skills and strategies and increase their general knowledge. All books are written, reviewed, and leveled for guided reading, early reading intervention, and Accelerated Reader™ programs for use in shared, guided, and independent reading and writing activities to support a balanced approach to literacy instruction. The SandCastle™ series has four levels that correspond to early literacy development. The levels are provided to help teachers and parents select appropriate books for young readers.

EMERGING • BEGINNING • TRANSITIONAL • FLUENT

CONTENTS

About Rain Forests — 4

Think About It — 22

Glossary — 24

ABOUT RAIN FORESTS

Tropical rain forests are very hot. They are **humid**.

They get a lot of rain.

Rain forests are full of life.

Many types of plants and animals live there.

Rain forest trees can be very tall. Some are 200 feet (61 m) high!

Many animals live in the tall treetops. Bats live there. Birds do too.

Other animals live in the **canopy**.

Snakes and frogs live there.
So do **sloths**.

Other plants grow near the ground. This area is called the understory.

Leopards live here.
So do many **insects**.

Insects also live on the rain forest floor. So do some spiders.

Gorillas live on the rain forest floor. Chimpanzees spend time there too.

Jane Goodall is a **primatologist**.

She works to **protect** chimpanzees and their **habitat**.

Rain forests are in danger. People cut down their trees.

They use them to make paper, furniture, and more.

It is important we **protect** rain forests. We can do this many ways!

Try to use less paper. Remember to recycle.

THINK ABOUT IT

Have you seen a rain forest on TV or in a book? What animals did you see?

GLOSSARY

canopy – the upper level of branches in a rain forest.

habitat – the area or environment where a person or animal usually lives.

humid – having a lot of moisture in the air.

insect – a small animal that has six legs and three main parts to its body.

primatologist – a person who studies primates such as humans, apes, or monkeys.

protect – to guard someone or something from harm or danger.

sloth – a type of mammal that lives in trees and moves very slowly.

tropical – located in the hottest areas on Earth.